ISBN 978-0-9955913-9-4

Alan Noake is a freelance IT consultant and qualified maths teacher who lives in the sticks near Sandwich in Kent. He is married. No kids. Alan has been a scout leader for over twenty-five years. He loves travelling and his big crazy dream is to visit Antarctica.

'Clerb2' is his second book about Clerb and the inhabitants of the planet Home almost 30 years later.

"Here's a test to find whether your mission on earth is finished: If you're alive it isn't."

Richard Bach,
from my perfect Desert Island Discs choice of book: "Illusions, The Adventures of a Reluctant Messiah".

for Andrea
(my HOME)

CLERB2

SECOND HOME:

More Crazy TIME Travel Adventures*

(*dairy free!)

by Alan S. Noake

BACKWARDS - FOREWORD (That's better!)

They say you should never go backwards in life and dwell in the past. Well I am making an exception! After about 30 years I think we all have a right to know if Clerb ever came back. Surely in this TIME of uncertainty and world crisis Clerb is needed more than ever. So here he is again just for the fun of it and just to ensure that trees everywhere have a right to be really bored once in a while again. Enjoy!

Alan S. Noake

Sandwich, Kent, 31st August 2017 on a wet Thursday afternoon - yes you guessed it - About Tea TIME. Make mine a nice cup of Darjeeling, you choose your favourite cuppa and off we go!

CLERB2 - 1

EVERYONE laughed. It was a deep, bellowing belly laugh which echoed across the years and the universe. How long had it been? Would it still work? Was it just a myth or an old wives' tale?

Bewtiffle stepped back in awe. Then he decided to step forward again for good measure. Was it too much to ask? He tried again, "Things on Gravel, I mean Earth, seem to be getting really bad indeed. Please help! It looks like they really need another Clerb."

EVERYONE took a long, ponderous moment to consider Bewtiffle's request. "You are just like your father was. When Uggerly had all those issues way back when with that Space Bus business, he pestered me and convinced me to create a Clerb. And remember what happened that TIME?!"

"Yes - Clerb helped to save the day. That's what happened. And when the day had been well and truly saved Clerb just up and vanished before we could even properly thank him," said Bewtiffle.

"But that's what Clerbs do. It is their sole reason to exist," stated EVERYONE. "And I get extremely exhausted aligning the stars, getting my ducks in a row and, for that matter, boring a whole bunch of trees just to make one happen. I don't even know if I am up to the challenge anymore."

Bewtiffle sulked. He drooped his head. He put on his finest dejected look and even grovelled a teeny bit. He knew that Earth needed another Clerb now more than ever before. He wished Uggerly was still alive. Uggerly would have known exactly what to do to get EVERYONE on board. Then it struck him. Ouch! All he had to do was use the old Sappleworth family magic... to raise EVERYONE's energy levels... the river Qwistle!

Bewtiffle now just had to figure out how to get a good glug of the almost dry liquid from the Qwistle into EVERYONE's morning cuppa without anyone, well specifically EVERYONE, noticing. It was going to involve a large bucket, some larger plastic pipe and an even larger amount of high quality stealth but he felt sure he could manage it. His father would have been really proud but of course wouldn't have told him so.

The next morning EVERYONE took a decent sip from his favourite mug - the one with "It's my universe, hand's off!" embossed in gold lettering around the side. He grinned, the grin turned into a smile, the smile turned into another deeper, bellowing-er, universe shattering laugh...

"TIME to really bore another tree," he exclaimed with enthusiastic conviction.

"Bewtiffle One - EVERYONE Nil." announced the umpire, a bit shocked at having entered the story so suddenly. He blinked and then made a hasty exit before he could fully establish why he had ever existed at all.

Clerb2 - 2

Clerb stood staring into the mirror. His single arm protruding from his belly waved a good morning wave - check. His hair covered his little stocky body all the way up to his forehead - check. He frowned - check. He got a really strong sense of Deja Vu - check, check. He could vaguely remember some branches and some distant leafy muttering on the lines of "I'm really bored with this." - check mate! But that's all he could remember. Nothing else. Now here he was just existing, looking at himself, wondering what his purpose was, wondering what he was supposed to do next?

Clerb sat down on a comfy couch and began to look around for inspiration. Eventually he found it in the form of an electronic tablet. He wasn't really sure what a tablet was but it looked sort of functional and well designed with a piece of half eaten fruit on the back. He picked it up and pressed the incredibly intuitive HOME button. The tablet beeped a couple of times and then a strangely familiar face appeared on the screen - the face of Bewtiffle Sappleworth.

"Clerb, I know you won't remember me, but I'm Bewtiffle."

'You're incredibly modest as well,' thought Clerb. But he was far too polite to say so. He just frowned a little at Bewtiffle and asked, "Where am I? Who am I? What is my purpose?"

"The first two questions I can answer quickly and easily Clerb", replied Bewtiffle. "However, the third one you will need to find out for yourself. You are on the planet Earth. You are a Clerb and to give you a little bit of a clue on the third question Clerbs exist because of a purpose. That's all I can say on that - if I told you your purpose on purpose you would become purposeless."

"So, I am here for a reason?", asked Clerb.

"Yes." said Bewtiffle.

"But you can't tell me the reason?", demanded Clerb.

"No." said Bewtiffle.

Clerb smiled. (Not good news for a Clerb.)

Clerb laughed. (Getting worse!)

Clerb held his sides to stop them from splitting with his arm. (Really dodgy ground now - and practically impossible with one arm!)

A red battery symbol blinked on the tablet screen and Bewtiffle's image flickered and distorted. "Find the white power cable and put this thing on charge Clerb", Bewtiffle just managed to say before the tablet screen just went black.

Clerb calmed himself down and assessed the situation. He thought long and hard. He finally decided he needed to explore so he looked around to find a door which showed promise. He bravely opened the door and stepped into a broom cupboard. He looked around for another door and this time he stepped outside. 'There has to be a purpose around here somewhere,' he thought to himself, as he took a breath of fresh air and set off along the street.

Clerb2 - 3

The planet Earth had certainly had its fair share of issues recently - disease, famine, war, terrorism, poverty, crime, economic disasters, natural disasters, unnatural disasters, climate change, pollution and back-dated PPI insurance claims. And in cosmic planet development terms it was actually only the 'Monday' of a planetary 'week'. In the grand scale of things EVERYONE had really messed this one up, big TIME. So, it was EVERYONE'S fault. There was no getting out of it EVERYONE was to blame.

Last time EVERYONE had created a Clerb for Uggerly things had certainly seemed a lot simpler back then. Nostalgic golden ages do have a habit of always seeming more simpler, more nostalgic and more golden but let's face it rescuing HOME from a nuisance Space Coach company certainly seems a lot easier in retrospect than the total mess EVERYONE had now created back on Earth. Could one Clerb really make a difference?

But whatever Bewtiffle had put in EVERYONE'S morning cuppa had finally convinced him to try. He at least felt compelled to take it all on and create a Clerb even if it felt entirely futile from the outset. And even if it made a teeny weeny bit of a difference it must be worth trying. Wasn't it?

Clerb2 - 4

Bert Trenchbottom was getting on a bit but the years had been kind to him. He had changed career immediately after all that 'weird alien yoghurt' fiasco ages ago. Bert was now a successful radiator salesman. He had actually got the idea from Bewtiffle. Bert concluded it would be a much more lucrative and rewarding career than security guarding in Sainsbury's. He was right. He loved selling radiators and literally bringing warmth into people's lives. Bert was a lot happier these days.

He often wondered what had happened to his old partner Ernest Wriggle. Ernest had gone a bit loopier than usual after the 'TIME travel experience' saga and had started yelling out yoghurt flavours in his sleep. Bert had completely lost touch with Ernest and thought it was probably for the best. (In fact, Ernest actually still worked back at Sainsbury's but was very careful to always avoid the yoghurt aisle.)

So, it was certainly a major surprise when Bert spotted Clerb walking directly towards him down the high street. 'Surely it couldn't be?' he thought to himself. "I'm hallucinating." But there was the little fellow just how Bert remembered him - stocky, hairy and single-armed with a big frown in his face. Incredible.

"Clerb!" shouted Bert.

But Clerb didn't recognise him at all. Clerb just gave a small frown and said, "Do I know you?"

"It was some TIME ago", explained Bert. "But we travelled through TIME in yoghurt together. Surely not something you could easily forget?" he asked.

"Sorry but I really don't remember", said Clerb. "You do seem vaguely familiar but yoghurt, TIME travel? Are you sure?"

"Let's go for a nice cup of tea, no yoghurts I promise, and I will tell you all about it." decided Bert.

"Accepted," said Clerb. "And perhaps you can also help me find my purpose?" He gave Bert an extra big frown.

Bert looked Clerb directly in the eyes and gave him the same advice Bewtiffle had given him via the tablet. "You will need to find out your purpose for yourself Clerb. I'm only a radiator salesman."

Clerb2 - 5

Stop right there! I have just about had enough of this...

.

.

.

.

[Long dramatic pause...]

.

.

.

.

[Even longer dramatic pause...]

.

.

.

.

[Followed by some silence...]

.

.

.

.

.

.

.

.

.

.

.

.

.

.

.

.

.

.

.

.

[And three more pauses each with another pause in the middle...]

.

.

.

.

.

[Ending in an extra special dramatic pause for effect...]

.

.

.

What's happened?

I am on strike.

'What do you mean you are on strike? You can't go on strike! You are the narrator!'

'So, who are you then?'

'I'm the author of course.'

'Exactly, you always get all the credit and no-one ever spares a moment to consider me. I'm the one who is stuck inside the book forever actually saying all the words. No-one ever gives me any awards or praise.'

'But you do get credit. It often says, Read by... you know who'

'THAT'S NOT THE NARRATOR! THAT'S ME.'

'Who the hell are you? said the narrator' **'and the author in unison.'**

'I'M THE AUDIO BOOK READER. I SPEND HOURS READING THE BLOODY THING AND HAVING TO READ BITS OF IT OVER AND OVER AGAIN BECAUSE THE AUDIO BOOK DIRECTOR MAKES ME GO ON AND ON UNTIL I GET IT JUST RIGHT.'

'But I exist without audio said the narrator. I exist in a magical place between page and reader. Without me this book would just vanish and not exist at all. Let me show you...'

[Another incredibly long, quite impressive and pretty irritating, paper-wasting dramatic pause...]

.

.

.

.

.

.

.

.

.

.

.

.

.

.

.

.

.

.

.

.

.

.

.

'Okay, okay point made' said the author.

'YES, ALRIGHT, WE GET WHERE YOU ARE COMING FROM' SAID THE AUDIO BOOK READER WHO WASN'T SURE WHICH FORMAT THE BOOK WAS CURRENTLY IN SO SAID IT ANY WAY.

So, here's to all the narrators. Let's celebrate them now. Without them the words just wouldn't make it off to the page at all and the main characters like Clerb just wouldn't get a look in. Raise a glass and toast narrators far and wide for all the great work they do for literature. There should be a new prize in the book world just for narrators and awarded each year to the narrator that makes the best job of narrating the narration...

'That's enough', said the author.

'YES, THAT'S DEFINITELY QUITE ENOUGH', SAID THE AUDIO BOOK READER (EVEN IN THE KINDLE FORMAT).

You are appreciated said EVERYONE.

Thanks guys! Strike over... I guess one of us can get back on with the story now... this narrating lark is all very good but I do ideally need to be told what to say occasionally...

Clerb2 - 6

Back on HOME Bewtiffle tried to calm down the rest of his fellow Homians. They were all gathered around in a gathering. Nighsley, Wickid and Horiblee all cheered to give him some encouragement to show their support.

"Thanks friends, that's all I can really say for now." He wasn't anywhere nearly as good at this public speaking lark as Uggerly had been but he did his best. "That's when the power ran out on Clerb's tablet and I lost contact but I think he got my key message about sorting out the human race and all the problems they have got themselves into lately.

Super-cringy-creep-creep put up his hand at the back of the crowd and the crowd parted to leave him standing there looking rather embarrassed.

"Yes, Super-cringy-creep-creep – you have a question?", asked Bewtiffle.

"Not so much of a question, just more of an observation really", said Super-cringy-creep-creep.

'There is always one!' thought Bewtiffle. 'And they are always in my gathered crowds', he continued to think to himself.

Super-cringy-creep-creep now looked even more embarrassed about his previous embarrassment but he did his best to make his point.

"Well," he started off nervously. "Medicine has now advanced significantly on Earth to eradicate most diseases soon; if human beings shared the food about a bit fairer they could certainly reduce famine; I would also suggest peace rather than war; they could try accepting each other's beliefs to put an end to terrorism; fight poverty; reduce crime; make the banks pay for any more economic disasters; target more resources at natural disasters; avert unnatural disasters; do whatever it is should already have been done but is still probably worth doing anyway to address climate change and, finally, bring down the levels of pollution by being a bit more sensible with things that pollute. That's just my opinion anyway but I don't really know what to suggest about solving the issue of back-dated PPI insurance claims."

The other Homians just stared at Super-cringy-creep-creep in disbelief. He certainly had a slightly more important cameo role in this story than he had in the past. He was a pretty dark horse indeed and had obviously been taking Earth's issues quite seriously indeed.

"Er, thank you Super-cringy-creep-creep," said Bewtiffle. "Now, where was I?"

"I think you had finished," said Nighlsey.

Clerb2 - 7

Clerb, on the other foot, had only just started. After a very pleasant cuppa and a chat with Bert who had updated him about his previous adventures he made his way back to his flat to see if the tablet had recharged sufficiently for him to resume his inter-galactic conversation with Bewtiffle.

Clerb now had to decide exactly what he should do next. Deciding to decide that had made him wish he had decided something a bit more decisive. He smiled and switched on the tablet.

This time there was no sign of Bewtiffle on the screen. After a few bleeps, it just showed a friendly colourful logo and an empty box with two plain grey buttons below – one button said 'SEARCH' and the other, you guessed it, "I'M FEELING LUCKY'. The choice was obvious really.

Clerb pressed the second button and the tablet presented him with a whole list of exciting options to help him on his quest for establishing his purpose.

"Blimey, that was extremely lucky", said Clerb. He scanned down the list weighing up the merits of each suggestion and making a mental note to revisit a few when he had more time.

The list read as follows...

I'M FEELING LUCKY

1204 RESULTS – PAGE 1 OF 121

1. **Meditate Daily** "Find inner peace and direction in your life by taking just 30 minutes every morning to..." *[www.meditatedaily.com]*
2. **Help Others** "Have you ever considered volunteering? Even just one evening a week..." *[www.helpothers.com]*
3. **Long Walks** "Troubles disappear on a long walk..." *[www.longwalks.com]*
4. **Eat Well** "A balanced diet will help you to live longer and take on the challenges of the day..." *[www.eatwell.com]*
5. **Work Hard** "Find solace in a meaningful career. Find your true calling ..." *[www.workhard.com]*
6. **Give to Charity** "A gift to others is really one to yourself..." *[www.givetocharity.com]*
7. **Travel Abroad** "Experiencing other cultures can help you find yourself..." *[www.travelabroad.com]*
8. **Read More** "A love of books is a love of life..." *[www.readmore.com]*
9. **Find Love** "You are never lost when you find a soul mate..." *[www.findlove.com]*
10. **Gone Home** "When your TIME finally comes don't be afraid to go on the next adventure..." *[www.gonehome.com]*

[Showing 1-10 of 1204 results] [Next]

Clerb studied the list for some time and clicked through a few more pages. He eventually concluded that being lucky itself was simply just a choice. He chose there and then to choose luck and picked a random number between 1 and 1204.

So Clerb chose randomly the top result on the third page #21 and decided that whatever it was it would at least half guide him towards his purpose. Not a very scientific approach he would have to admit but he felt that Earth had enough really good science right now and it desperately needed something much more non-scientific! He felt that in a world of advanced technology and scientific breakthroughs certain simple important things were getting very lost. Mankind was beginning to wonder where they had put them! And Clerb's purpose must be to help them to find them again, whatever they were.

Clerb decided to start with Bert and Ernest. He sped out of the flat with fresh enthusiasm and a good dose of now knowing exactly which direction he was heading in - Sainsbury's.

Yes - Ernest Wriggle was still there after all these years. He had the grey hairs to show for it. One for every disagreeable customer he had ever had to deal with and a bunch more for dealing with that unmentionable 'yoghurt affair'. He still lived with Miz (couldn't cope without her!) but the kids - Elly and Jess - had long since left home and started upon life's journey of collecting grey hairs of their own.

Ernest scanned the bank of security cameras. Nothing out of the ordinary - just shoppers going about their shopping innocently shopping for things. Empty aisles of cans and packages; the fish counter; the Martian; the meat counter; the bakery... rewind! The Martian! No, it couldn't be! But the image wasn't in his imagination. There just by the pickles and sauces was... well it just had to be... but why...? Frowning up at the security camera and waving directly at Ernest was Clerb.

Ernest shuddered. He didn't know if his nerves could take it. He blinked a few times just to make sure but Clerb was still there and just wouldn't be imagined away for anybody. Ernest had spent years in therapy. He tried one of the breathing techniques the therapist had taught him and still found himself gasping for breath. He finally mustered enough courage to get out of his seat and make his way down to the supermarket floor.

"Is it really you Clerb?" he asked.

"Indeed, it is", replied Clerb. "Quick follow me!"

"Where are we going?" demanded Ernest and growing a little in confidence. "I am not sure if I can cope with any more TIME travel Clerb."

Clerb led him out into the car park and tried to flag down the first taxi arriving to pick up shoppers. The taxi driver could only see Ernest behaving strangely as if he was salsa dancing while drunk. Anyway, he opened the door and watched while Ernest paused briefly before jumping in through the open cab door.

"Where to squire?", requested the cabby.

"Tell him to take us to the Hothouse Radiators showrooms", whispered Clerb settling in the back seat next to him.

"Er, Hothouse showrooms on Froggit Lane please", Ernest informed the cabby. The cabby set off obligingly without delay and Ernest sank back into his seat to gather his thoughts.

Before long Clerb and Ernest were standing right in front of the showrooms. Clerb stopped in his tracks when he noticed a very strange yellow golden oddly shaped cloud hovering immediately above the showrooms. He felt very odd himself but just shook his head and ignored it.

Then leaving Ernest behind Clerb went straight inside without delay and located Bert. "There is someone outside who wants to see you", explained Clerb. "It is really important that you make friends again and accept each other for who you are."

Bert followed Clerb back to the open door.

Bert looked at Ernest, nervously.

Ernest looked back at Bert and strained a smile.

Clerb looked at them both, with an 'excited' frown.

This was going to take a while but it was an extremely good start.

Clerb2 - 8

EVERYONE felt a tiny tremor in the fabric of the universe. At first, he thought it might have just been something he had eaten but then he realised that it was indeed a 'Clerbic' reaction. It was something he hadn't experienced for nearly thirty years but he was absolutely sure that Clerb had actually made a start on finding his true purpose.

From his vantage point, EVERYONE could see and feel anywhere in the universe. And there in the distance coming from Earth the Clerbic reaction showed up as two tiny fluorescent green dots merging to form a slightly larger tiny fluorescent green dot. "Crikey," said EVERYONE. "It's working!"

'That #21 really is a very effective Clerbic experiment', he thought. And he double checked the top of page 3 of his 'I'M FEELING LUCKY' system...

21. **Value Friendships** "Make and keep friends. Friendship is the glue that holds the universe together..."
[www.valuefriendships.com]

.

.

.

EVERYONE knew he was on to something. He decided to pop back to HOME and meet up again with his friend Bewtiffle for a progress meeting.

They sat down by the banks of the Qwistle and watched the very slow ripples heave their way along the surface like reluctant children making their way to school.

"I told you Earth needed a Clerb", said Bewtiffle arrogantly.

"Yes," EVERYONE admitted. "You were right." He didn't often admit to being wrong but he was prepared to do so for Bewtiffle.

"So what next? asked Bewtiffle. "One Clerbic reaction is not just going to solve the world's problems, is it?" he said rhetorically.

So, EVERYONE told him the starfish story. You know the one...

There was an old man on a beach picking up starfish. But the beach was covered with millions upon millions of starfish all washed up and dying in the heat of the sun. A young boy walked up to the old man and said, "You are never, ever going to make a difference!". The old man looked at the young man. Then he picked up another starfish and threw it back into the sea. "Made a difference to that one!", he said.

Bewtiffle sat staring at the river and smiled. He now understood what needed to be done. He just needed to find a way to get to Earth and help Clerb. There were still a great many 'starfish' to save and now they just needed to find a catalyst to make the Clerbic reaction go viral.

Bewtiffle called together his fellow Homians once more and even more confidently addressed the crowd.

"Elders of Oldar", he began. "Clerb has found a way to help Earth but he will really need our help."

Horyblee shouted out what the rest of the Homians were thinking. "This is not going to involve anyone getting immersed in weird flavours of Yoghurt again is it Bewtiffle?"

"I do hope not," replied Bewtiffle. "I think EVERYONE has found a dairy-free way for some of us to get to Earth. But it will still mean travelling through TIME and space. And it will also mean you run the risk of being an entirely different random age on your return if you do volunteer to come."

"Count me in," said Terryblee. He really fancied coming back older than his twin brother Horyblee for a change!

"Yes, I'm in too", said Konsiderat considerately.

So that now made it Bewtiffle, Horyblee, Terryblee, and Konsiderat. Along with Whickid and Nighsley who also stepped forward they formed a humble gang of six Homians ready to go to Earth.

"But you will also need a mission name," shouted out Super-cringy-creep-creep. "How about Second Home?" he suggested.

"I like it said Bewtiffle," it is very fitting. "Second Home it is then." He called out to EVERYONE who could have heard him from anywhere.

"There is no need to shout," said EVERYONE. "Okay are you all ready for this?"

The Second Home gang of six all nodded at once.

From out of nowhere a golden six-seater peddle cart appeared with a sun canopy over it and the number plate SH1 (for 'Second Home One').

"Really lucky you didn't name it the 'Second Home One Transporter' or something else beginning with T!" exclaimed Whickid chuckling privately to himself and imagining that number plate instead.

The gang of six all boarded the peddle cart and started pedalling frantically. The cart simply disappeared from HOME as quickly as it had arrived.

Clerb2 – 9 – INTERMISSION

'Let's take a moment to all have a break and reflect on the story so far.' suggested the narrator.

'Great idea.' said the author. 'I don't know about you but I am ready for another cuppa.'

'I COULD DO WITH SOMETHING A BIT STRONGER' SAID THE AUDIO BOOK READER. 'GOT ANY VODKA?'

'We don't want you drunk in charge of an audio book!' the narrator snapped back. 'You would ruin it!'

'BUT IT HELPS ME TO RELAX AND DO ALL THE SILLY VOICES' SAID THE AUDIO BOOK READER.

'But I don't want to be read in a silly voice, my narration should be taken seriously.' the narrator narrated.

'Look while you two are arguing about it I am off to put the kettle on.' said the author. 'Do you both want a cuppa or not?'

'OH ALRIGHT, BETTER THAN NOTHING I SUPPOSE, ALL THIS READING OUT LOUD DOES MAKE MY THROAT DRY.' SAID THE AUDIO BOOK READER.

'Oh, go on then,' said the narrator. 'Two sugars in mine... and then we really must press on. I am dying to know what happens next.'
'But I haven't written it yet!' said the author.

'And so, the author went off to make three large mugs of tea,' continued the narrator. 'And until he gets his skates on and comes back I am afraid I won't be able to carry on with the story...'

'ME NEITHER' SAID THE AUDIO BOOK READER.
.
.
.
.
.
.
.
.
.
.
.
.
.
.
.
.
.
.

.
.
.
.

'Okay, tea is served gentlemen', now back to the pot, I mean, plot' said the author refreshed and ready for more authoring.

Clerb2 – 10

TIME had been enjoying a nice afternoon nap.

He never normally had a break from himself but every now and again things seemed to grind to a halt. If he wasn't very busy he infrequently got a moment just to put his feet up.

On this occasion TIME had waited years, months, weeks, days, hours and even a few seconds before having a break. He had finally laid down on a recliner hidden at the bottom of his garden and drifted off into oblivion...

So, it was more than a tad annoying when less than 30 seconds later he was rudely interrupted...

There was a flash of gold.

There was a sound of very energetic pedalling.

TIME began to get one of his tension headaches again. He jumped into action and simultaneously reached out his thoughts into parts of the universe he didn't even know existed before.

The six very old Homians on their golden pedal car suddenly appeared hovering about 50 metres above the Earth without realising they had spoilt TIME's afternoon off. TIME went to try to lay back down for a rest again but he was now troubled and couldn't relax. He did have a relentless habit of going on.

From the yellow cloud that surrounded the pedal car Bewtiffle and his friends could see a building below. As they peered through the golden mist they saw a taxi pull up in front of the building.

They all watched as Clerb and Ernest stepped out of the taxi onto the forecourt. Then Clerb seemed to spend ages explaining something to Ernest. Ernest proceeded to get extremely upset and before Clerb could stop him he had made his way back to the taxi. The taxi sped off into the distance and Clerb just stood there. At first Clerb started to smile and then he started laughing hysterically at the top of his voice. He had obviously thought this was going to be easy. After all Bert and Ernest had been partners once – how could he ever fulfil his purpose if he couldn't reunite those two!

Whickid was the first to say something. "So, what do we do now?" he asked the others in the pedal car. He wasn't expecting an answer.

"Down there on Earth it hasn't actually happened yet." They all jumped in shock when they heard the bellowing voice of EVERYONE. "I need your help to cause the Clerbic reaction we witnessed from HOME."

Bewtiffle tried to comprehend what EVERYONE meant. "So, you are saying that the Clerbic reaction hasn't actually happened here yet but we actually witnessed it?"

"I know," said EVERYONE. "Confusing isn't it. TIME sometimes has a habit of confusing people and he has really been getting ahead of himself lately. So, each of you has just one chance to change the course of events. Someone needs to go back in TIME to warn Clerb before he and Ernest even get into the taxi.

"The minor catch is that I can't guarantee when in TIME each of you will go. So, who is willing to go first?"

"Okay, let's get it over with," said Konsiderat after a few moments of careful consideration. "So what do I do?"

"Simply start pedalling while the rest of you stay perfectly still," said EVERYONE.

Somehow Konsiderat just cycled off out of the pedal car on a normal two-wheel bike. Well, I say normal, the two-wheel bike was still made of solid gold!

Clerb2 – 11 – Considerately Done

The melodic tones of 'Search Light Rag' by Scott Joplin which was playing on the Pedal car's radio faded away behind him as Konsiderat cycled smoothly down to Earth and seemed to be approaching a small island close to a wide harbour near the coast. Although he was very old he found the bicycle easy to pedal. Konsiderat finally brought the bike to a standstill and started to explore the island's paths and forested areas. Where could he be? More importantly when could he be?

A tall, smart military man appeared from out of the trees. He saw Konsiderat and immediately rushed over to shake his hand. "How do you do my good man? Pleased to meet you, my name is Lieutenant General Robert Stephenson Smyth Baden-Powell. Try saying all that with your teeth in, hey? And who might you be? You are not from these parts that's for certain."

"I'm Konsiderat" replied Konsiderat. He didn't know who this… "What did you say your name was again?"

"Just call me B-P. All the boys on the experimental camp do!" said B-P in a cheery fashion.

"Er, okay, B-P. Do you mind me asking where we are and, more embarrassingly, when we are? That is, what year it is?"

"This is Brownsea. But surely you know that? We are just out from Poole Harbour. But the year well it is August 1907 – now why on Earth wouldn't you know the year. You look like you have seen quite a few of 'em?"

Konsiderat warmed to this old war hero. He somehow felt he could trust him with the truth. "1907, oh dear, I seem to be over a hundred years out. Well, here goes, I am a Homian from the planet HOME and I was trying to find Clerb to help him cause a Clerbic reaction."

"Woah, stop right there, did you say planet? You are from another planet? And what may I ask is a Clerb?"

"Sorry, I guess I better start right at the beginning." said Konsiderat.

"Very sensible my man," remarked B-P. He sat and kindly listened intently and nodded while Konsiderat told him the whole story.

When Konsiderat was done and had finally paused for breath B-P looked at him and said, "Well I wouldn't use quite the same language, Clerbs indeed, but I do think my little experiment with the boys here on Brownsea is just like trying to start a Clerbic reaction. We are teaching them all about camping, observation, woodcraft, chivalry, lifesaving and patriotism. I would love to see these teachings spread all around the world one day."

Konsiderat liked this old Lieutenant General and even though he had missed warning Clerb by years he felt that his attempt wasn't entirely wasted. Maybe even if it just sent a ripple down through the years to Clerb? It might make a difference.

It was obviously TIME for B-P to return to his camp as he shook Konsiderat's hand and then turned to walk away back into the woods. Konsiderat felt that he too should return and go back to the golden cloud to give one of the other Homians a chance to warn Clerb.

By the TIME B-P looked back all he could see was a wonderful golden sunrise. He made a mental note of the date – the 1st of August 1907. A date to truly remember. "Heavens, there I go," he chuckled to himself. "I've must have been day-dreaming again. Konsiderat, Konsiderat indeed...?"

"Of course! A Scout is to be friendly and Konsiderat..." said B-P muttering to himself as he marched away. "That's it. That can be the other part of my third Scout law – considerate! Ripping! I'll use that! It follows, that the real way to get happiness is by giving out happiness to other people. Friendly and considerate – that just sums it up perfectly."

Clerb2 – 12 – Beautifully Done

"I'm sick of this old music!" said Bewtiffle just as Konsiderat arrived back to the pedal car. Bewtiffle spun the radio dial round as far as it would go. A strange techno-beat unlike anything they had all heard before started to play. "Now this is more like it," shouted Bewtiffle. "If you want something done, you've got to do it yourself." He cycled off confidently.

But it wasn't long before he knew he was too late. Possibly many years too late?! He seemed to be in the correct area of London but the city now looked something like it must have done back in the Blitz. Something was very wrong indeed...

Bewtiffle parked the bike against a wall that now looked much shorter than it should be. What was he going to do? Two teenage boys just walked by swearing and ignored him. In the distance, he heard a strange noise. So, with no better clues as to what to do next he decided to go and find out what was causing all the commotion.

Bewtiffle made his way through the bleak dystopian streets. 'I know nostalgia really isn't what it used to be but this is ridiculous,' he thought. The evidence was all around him – the city was soulless. 'Times really were more golden for Earth last time I was here. Absolutely no doubt about that.'

Bewtiffle turned a corner and was dumbfounded by what he found dumbly in the public square. For a start, there were pigeons everywhere! He knew last TIME he was on planet Earth there were no longer thousands of pigeons flocking for little tubs of seed sold in this square. Secondly, the guy on top of the pillar wearing the admiral's hat was 50% missing. A half Nelson? Thirdly, the giant lions looked all emaciated – they had certainly seen better days. It was a depressing sight indeed and there sitting in one of the water fountains was Clerb shouting at the top of his voice.

Clerb looked up woefully with a grin as Bewtiffle approached. He recognised his old friend but looked all smiley and was obviously embarrassed to see him. He had a pigeon on each shoulder pecking at his ears. Clerb looked a shocking state.

"What's happened to this place Clerb? I hardly recognise it," stated Bewtiffle.

"I know," answered Clerb. "I failed Bewtiffle. I no longer have a purpose. I am purposeless and suffering from severe purposeless-ness."

"TIME and EVERYONE is also to blame Clerb," said Bewtiffle, trying to reassure Clerb. "You can't take responsibility for this all on your shoulders."

At the mention of "shoulders" the two pigeons either side of Clerb stopped pecking at him and took flight. "I know said Clerb," beaming with despair. "But if I had just managed to get Bert and Ernest back together as friends again I feel things could have been very different."

Clerb stepped out of the fountain and shook himself down. His hairy body dried quickly in the midday sun. He sat down with Bewtiffle on the rim of the fountain and they both stared out at the flocks of pigeons.

"I've failed too," said Bewtiffle. "But there is some hope Clerb. What I can tell you is there is still a four out of six, two-thirds, chance of this future not happening. Now those are pretty good odds by any standards of oddness, yes?"

Clerb frowned a little. A glimmer of hope. "What a beautiful day," he said. "After years of hopelessness." But this Clerb also realised that if Bewtiffle was correct then this version of himself wouldn't ever have existed. It was a strange feeling – but to achieve his purpose he would never be here right now. He frowned deeply – it was worth it.

Bewtiffle got up to return to his bike a few streets away. "I'll see you in another TIME Clerb," he said as he walked off, without looking back, on purpose.

Clerb2 – 13 – Horribly and Terribly Done

"It's TIME for the twins to have a go," said EVERYONE.

Mysteriously on the radio, there was now a reading from Spearshake the great Homian playwright...

"The TIME is out of joint—O cursèd spite,
That ever I was born to set it right!
Nay, come, let's go together."

Hamlet Act 1, scene 5, 188-190

"Yes, let's go together!" said Horriblee.

"Once more unto the breach," exclaimed Terriblee.

They cycled out from the pedal car on a golden tandem. "Watch out for ice!", shouted Bewtiffle, ever helpful.

The London winter streets were extremely icy. They were in the right place but just over 400 years too early! The tandem skidded to a halt outside a Southwark ale house.

"Fancy a beer?" asked Horriblee.

"It would be rude not too," replied Terriblee.

They parked the golden tandem right outside the ale house and went through the large oak door. Sitting around the bar were a mix of characters - all chatting, singing and drinking.

At the bar, on a bar stool, sat a friendly young man wearing a white ruff around his neck. He looked up when Horriblee and Terriblee came through the oak door.

"We came into the world like brother and brother, And now let's go hand in hand, not one before another," quipped the young man off the cuff. "That's good," he muttered reassuringly to himself. "That's really good. I can use that."

"But that's a Spearshake quote," shouted Terriblee. "You're out of line claiming that line as your own."

"Yes, you've really crossed the line there sir," backed up Horriblee.

"Spearshake, Spearshake, who is this imposter of which you speak? Do you know who I am my good man? My name is William Shakespeare and I intend to be the greatest playwright in Southwark one day."

"Three beers barman," requested Terriblee. 'This was going to be fun' he thought. A young confident drunk upstart crow who thinks he is going places. "Would I were in an alehouse in London," he bawled with delight.
"Can I borrow that line for a penny?" said Shakespeare. "I can use that."

"Be my guest," said Terriblee. "Nothing can come of nothing."

"Oh, you are good! I'll use that too if you don't mind – 'Nothing can come of nothing' I doth like it much."

"Does he get another penny?" asked Horriblee ensuring they could afford the inevitable next round.

"Does he get another penny? No, can't really use that." decided Shakespeare flippantly. "Where are you twins from? Illyria? Messaline? You are not from these parts."

"We are Homians from the planet HOME..." began Terriblee.

"Barman, three more tankards of your finest ale" demanded Shakespeare. "I can tell this is going to be an inspirational afternoon's work. Do go on. We shall all three be as merry as the day is long."

"You can use that!", screeched the two brothers.

Shakespeare watched as the two brothers finally walked back to the old oak door. "Unbidden guests are often welcomest when they are gone," he exclaimed. "Ooh, I can use that too," he chuckled.

Clerb2 – 14 – Wickedly Done

"Okay, I guess it is TIME for my Quest now" said Whickid. "So what music do I get to make a dramatic entrance with?"

Bewtiffle spun the dial round again to 192.1 FM and heard the sounds of Isham Jones and his Orchestra playing the Wabash Blues...

"Oh, those Wabash Blues
I know I got my dues
A lonesome soul am I
I feel that I could die

Candle light that gleams
Taunts me in my dreams
I'll pack my walking shoes
To lose those Wabash Blues"

"I'll pack my walking shoes," echoed Whickid and he also cycled down into London. "To lose those Wabash Blues."

The bike came to a standstill on the stern of a ship sailing down the Thames under Tower Bridge and off out to sea. Whickid left the bike at the stern lent against the cabin wall and wandered round to see what all the commotion was on the bow of the ship.

Ernest Shackleton and his crew were gathered on deck for a photo shoot. The camera recorded all the men having a flag ceremony including two older scouts who had joined the expedition – James Marr and Norman Mooney.

Whickid carefully kept out of the photos and filming. He didn't want to upset TIME too much. It was bad enough he was still one hundred years too early to warn Clerb.

"Who do we have here?" Ernest Shackleton demanded. "A stowaway, no doubt? What do you have to say for yourself? Trying to join our Quest Expedition?"

"Well, er," stuttered Whickid. "Quest? That's weird. Anyway, if I told you, you wouldn't believe me and to be honest I am not really sure why I here at all myself. But I must be here for a reason."

James Marr one of the scouts came up to join the two of them and asked, "Is there a problem boss?"

"This chap...", Shackleton started.

"Whickid." finished Whickid.

"Very wicked indeed," said Shackleton. "I've a good mind to make him walk the plank."

"How did you get here?" the Scout Marr queried. "The truth please. A scout is to be trusted."

"It's a very long story." said Whickid. 'Didn't Konsiderat ramble on about Scouts or something?' he thought to himself. 'Something about the beginning of another Clerbic type reaction?'

"Well we've got an extremely long voyage ahead of us," said Shackleton. "And the chaps like a good yarn."

But Whickid just knew he had to get back to lose those Wabash Blues.

"I am sorry gentlemen but I'm on my bike!" shouted Whickid running to the stern of the ship.

"I didn't think he meant it literally" stated Shackleton.

"Nice chap Sir," said Scout Marr.

"Did that really just happen?" asked Shackleton.

"I think so boss", replied Marr. "But I am beginning to doubt it myself."

"Oh well!" said Shackleton, "Spirits up boy! A man must shape himself to a new mark directly the old one goes to ground."

"I'm honoured to be considered your friend boss", said Marr. "Let's begin this Quest".

Clerb2 – 15 – Nicely Done

"I've got it! screamed Nighsley excitedly. "I have sat here all this time waiting and listening while you have all had a go. But I've got it! I know exactly how to get to Clerb in TIME."

He leaned forward and tuned the radio to 201.7 FM. "Let's just hope I do arrive in TIME."

"Don't worry, you'll be spot on, I'll make sure of it," said TIME.

"Where have you been all this TIME, TIME?" demanded Bewtiffle.

"Right here, just been waiting for the right music", TIME replied. "Now let's get cracking!"

The Pedal car radio blared out the sound of Ed Sheeran singing Shape of You...

"... Tell the driver make the radio play, and I'm singing like. Girl, you know I want your love. Your love was

handmade for somebody like me. Come on now, follow my lead..."

I was wondering when someone would finally work it out said EVERYONE. "Now, follow my lead...!"

"Nicely done, Nighsley!" rejoiced the other everyone (the other five Homians).
Nighsley pedalled down to Earth as fast as he possibly could. The pressure was on. He knew he had TIME on his side now but he still needed EVERYONE to help him warn Clerb.

'I need to get to Clerb before he jumps into the taxi with Ernest' Nighsley concluded to himself. He abandoned his bike and ran down the High Street. Nighsley was a Homian on a mission. It was odd but even though the odds of success were dropping rapidly he felt that things had all been so odd already that it was TIME for something really odd to happen. He wasn't wrong.

Walking towards him up the High Street was, well, himself. Nighsley took a step backwards in shock. He stared at this other version of himself. 'I'm pretty good looking for 642' he thought vainly.

The other Nighsley also stopped in his tracks and smiled, you guessed it, nicely. "You've done it," he said. "Congratulations!" Then the other Nighsley just walked on by with a hop, skip and a jump and disappeared into the distance.

"I've done what?" wondered Nighsley. Stunned to see yet another version of himself on the other side of the road smiling at him. He couldn't cope with all this excessive nice-ness. This TIME he decided to ignore 'himself' press on and find Clerb.

As he reached Clerb's flat he heard EVERYONE's voice booming dramatically for good effect in his ears.

"You are our final hope Nighsley. Don't let us down! All you have to do is convince Clerb that he mustn't tell Ernest that they were going to meet with Bert before Clerb has spoken to Bert first."

But Clerb wasn't in? Nighsley knocked on the flat door again. No answer at all, not even a confused hippie appeared. He must be too late?

"Damn," said TIME. I seem to have fallen asleep for a few minutes. "Now, where was I?"

Nighsley made his way as quickly as he could back to his golden bike. He was no experienced cyclist but he pedalled off in the direction of Hothouse Radiators as fast as he could. He could soon see the taxi up ahead. Inside he could just make out the figures of Clerb and Ernest. But he just couldn't catch up.

EVERYONE stepped in to help. TIME stopped for EVERYONE. TIME hadn't stopped for Nighsley. He cycled up to the side of the now weirdly stationary moving taxi. He leapt off his bike and opened the rear nearside passenger door. Clerb popped his head out and frowned. "What do you want Nighsley?"

"Boy am I pleased to see you?" said Nighsley rhetorically. "We really need to talk."

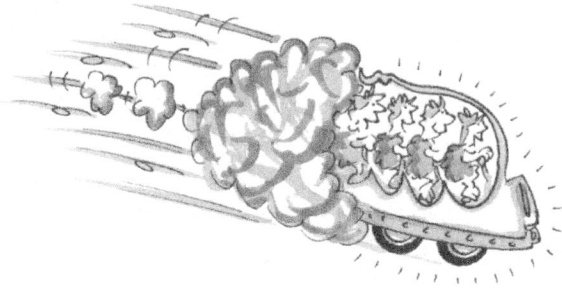

Clerb2 - 16

Before long Clerb and Ernest were standing right in front of the showrooms. Clerb stopped in his tracks when he noticed a very strange yellow golden oddly shaped cloud hovering immediately above the showrooms. He felt very odd himself but just shook his head and ignored it.

Then leaving Ernest behind Clerb went straight inside without delay and located Bert. "There is someone outside who wants to see you", explained Clerb. "It is really important that you make friends again and accept each other for who you are."

Bert followed Clerb back to the open door.

Bert looked at Ernest, nervously.

Ernest looked back at Bert and strained a smile.

Clerb looked at them both, with an 'excited' frown.

This was going to take a while but it was an extremely good start and very nicely done.

Then suddenly flying out of the yellow oddly shaped cloud came a golden pedal car full of Homians gliding down in front of the friendly group of three friends – Clerb, Bert and Ernest.

Clerb2 – 17

Clerb knew with certainty it was TIME to go again.

Bert, Ernest, Bewtiffle, Horyblee, Terryblee, Konsiderat, Whickid and Nighsley (feeling all smug) all gathered around Clerb somehow knowing too that it was that TIME. EVERYONE was there.

Clerb frowned and shrugged his shoulders. He could be proud. After all he had started something fun and good – a kind of Second HOME here on Earth. He hoped that it would spread like a huge chain reaction around the world – one friendship after another. Each one building on the last one. Each reconciliation adding to the initial Clerbic reaction. Each friendly handshake or heart-warming hug spreading to the next one and the next one until finally there was no-one left unhugged. One big world embracing hug – now wouldn't that be good?

If it worked Clerb thought, no trees would ever have to be bored again and with that final thought lingering in the air Clerb vanished.

.

.

.

.

"Now how on <u>Earth</u> are we going to get HOME?" asked Bewtiffle.

Clerb2 - AFTERWORDS

'CAN I STOP NOW?' SAID THE AUDIO BOOK READER. 'MY THROAT IS REALLY SORE.'

'Oh, stop complaining.' said the narrator. 'Doing all my stuff gives me a migraine.'

'Do you two ever stop moaning?' demanded the author. 'I have just had to say goodbye once again to my favourite character and all you two can do is moan, moan, moan,..'

'NOW THAT GOT A REACTION!'

'WHO SAID THAT?' ASKED THE AUDIO BOOK READER.

'Wasn't me.' said the narrator.

'Or me?' said the author confused. 'You couldn't write this stuff.'

'You obviously didn't write this stuff!' exclaimed the narrator.

'DOES THAT MEAN WE CAN STOP NOW?' GASPED THE AUDIO BOOK READER.

'And, so they all went HOME.' finished the narrator.

CLERB GONE HOME (AGAIN)

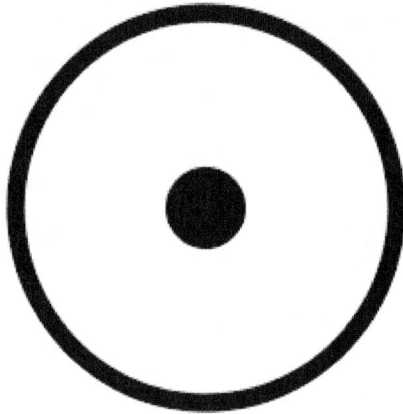

Printed in Great Britain
by Amazon